JERRY

His journey led him from the heart of the mysterious Time Centre, and a past too incredible to be real, across the steppes of a strangely altered China—and into a future beyond imagination. Also known as Elric, Asquiol, Clovis Marca, now and forever he was Jerry Cornelius, the eternal champion...

THE CORNELIUS CHRONICLES

"He is a superhero, ex-clergyman, ex-politician, physicist, spy, and card-carrying satyr on a rampage through the welts and crevices of time...an antic, vibragun-toting womanizer of the highest order."
The Washington Post

"A modern myth character living in a fantasy world—a new messiah who doesn't let himself be ruled by inevitability."
New Scientist

Other Avon Books by
Michael Moorcock

BREAKFAST IN THE RUINS
THE CORNELIUS CHRONICLES

Coming Soon
THE CORNELIUS CHRONICLES, VOL. III